THE MIDNIGHT WOMBAT OF
MOODONG CREEK
A YELLOWSTONE LEGEND

Kerry Anne Boer

Nannakaz Chronicles

This Book Belongs To

To the wild ones of Moodong Creek -
who move unseen along ridgelines and
hollow logs,
who carve flight into sky and claw into bark,
who drink where moonlight spills silver on
still water.

To those who knew the valley before fences,
and keep its secrets in feather, fur, and scale.

To the wombat, the wallaby, the lace
monitor,
and all the untamed kin who remind us the
earth is not ours alone.

Your paths are paw-prints of eternity.

Your voices thread the wind.

In reverence, in wonder, in kinship

About the author

Kerry Anne Boer is an author, storyteller, and dedicated Rememberer-in-Residence whose works blend imagination, history, and the gentle whispers of nature. Deeply inspired by the landscapes and legends of the Australian bush, she weaves together truth and fantasy, giving voice to stories that might otherwise remain hidden in the shadows of the past.

Her latest book, The Midnight Wombat of Moodong Creek, is inspired by the wild Australian landscape she grew up exploring, where granite banks, whispering creeks, and hidden creatures shaped her love for storytelling.

When she is not writing, Kerry Anne can often be found wandering creeks and valleys, notebook in hand, listening carefully to what the She Oaks have to share. She lives on a farm nestled in the historic Yellowstone Estate in New South Wales, surrounded by family, beloved animals, and, of course, whispering trees.

To discover more about Kerry Anne's stories or to explore her other Artworks, please visit her website at **https://www.kerryanneboer.com.au** or follow her adventures on social media **@kerryanneboer**

These days, she finds inspiration while gently swinging in an egg chair under the shade of a Moonlight Grevillia tree in her fairy garden, with her loyal border collie curled up nearby.

Also by Kerry Anne Boer

"Chemo Sunrise: A Poetic & Picturesque Journey"

Buried Treasures Series

"Mum & Me At The Hippy Campus"
"Me & The Buried Art of Thinking Differently"
"Me & Naughty Fridays"

Cosmic Connections Series

"Moon Meow"
"Once In A Bogong Blue Moon"

Nannakaz Chronicles

"The Whispering Trees of Yellowstone"

The valley holds its stories close,

In whispered leaves and creek-side sighs.

Where stones keep warmth like memories,

And gentle winds breathe lullabies.

She Oaks guard forgotten dreams,

Their branches weave the past to now.

Roots reach deep to ancient truths,

The land recalls each whispered vow.

Between the quiet and the song,

The shadows bloom, the sunlight stirs.

Names grow softly, patiently,

Awaiting hearts to call them hers.

Here the valley waits and listens,

Holding safe each echoed word.

For what was lost, returns again,

And what is silent, still is heard.

Introduction

This story began with a shadow... Not the kind that hides, but the type that waits - quiet, patient, and ancient as the stones themselves. Not far from the She Oaks, where Moodong Creek curves like a silver thread, lies a steep red crushed granite bank. In its depths, in its hollows, in its midnight silences, something stirs.

The Midnight Wombat of Moodong Creek grows from deep earth - some remembered, some imagined, all belonging. At its heart lies the Yellowstone Estate once more, in valleys carried by history and hushed by time. It is a place where voices echo not only in branches, but also in burrows, in the steady tread of paws beneath the soil, in the secret chambers where crystals hum with memory.

This story belongs to the hidden keepers, the quiet guardians who dig unseen and know the ground as others know the sky. The wombat is one such keeper, and though his journey may appear stitched from wonder, his path is as real as the roots that bind the land. Moodong Creek flows, carrying whispers from one valley to the next, from one story to another, weaving all into a single song.

Here, fantasy and truth walk side by side. A hoofbeat, a pawprint, a whisper, a name - all are part of the valley's remembering. If you listen closely, you may feel the pulse of the soil, steady and sure, guiding you toward mysteries older than memory itself.

As you journey deeper, you'll find that not all connections are of this world. Some belong to stone, to shadow, to midnight silence. And yet they shape us, as surely as the sun shapes the morning.

Welcome back to Yellowstone. The wombat is waiting. The creek is calling. The midnight hour has come.

With warmth and wonder,

Kerry Anne Boer

Author & Rememberer-in-Residence

Contents

The Meadow and the Horses

The wildflower meadow lies like a quilt across the slope, stitched in gold, violet, and blue. The She Oaks at its edge breathe their secrets into the breeze, their whispers threading down toward Moodong Creek. Granite stones soak the morning sun, warm as resting hands. Every sound belongs - the hum of bees, the hush of grass, the soft thud of hooves.

It is morning, and the meadow is awake. Dragonflies dart above the creek, their wings flashing silver-green. A pink finch-cloud bursts from the fence line, scattering like sparks. Ants march in long lines over the granite, carrying crumbs too heavy for their size. Everything here moves with purpose, yet everything seems at rest, as though the valley is in no hurry at all to reveal its secrets.

Three horses rule as though it were their very own kingdom.

Thelma and Louise - pintos with patches bright as spilled milk - gallop through the valley together, tails snapping, manes streaming like banners. Their strides never quite match, one leaping ahead, the other lagging behind, then swapping as though they cannot decide who should lead. Their hooves drum the earth until the bees rise in a hum of protest.

Sapphire follows along at a sensible distance. Her coat is the color of baked earth, her glacier eyes holding a silence older than her years. She does not race or quarrel. She moves as if the meadow itself bends to make way for her, calm and confident, her hooves steady as her heartbeat.

If you stand still long enough, the meadow will tell you what the horses are thinking. It begins like the rustle of grass, like a whisper half-carried by the wind.

Thelma's eyes shine toward the fence line, where yesterday's apples rolled loose from a forgotten basket. The word gleams with her gaze: Apples.

Louise stamps a hoof, and the ground itself seems to echo: Carrots.

The two of them are never still, never silent - two queens forever quibbling over treasure. Their quarrels ripple through the air until the She Oaks seem to chuckle, their whispers bending lower as if to listen.

Sapphire does not answer. Her silence is heavier than words, a pause that seems to stretch down into the soil itself. Yet in that pause is something firm, something unyielding. She knows what she loves, though she need not say it.

Thelma tosses her mane, gleefully. Apples shine, her voice insists. Louise stamps again, stubborn. Carrots crunch. The quarrel builds until the two pintos lunge into a chase, circling the meadow in flashing arcs of white and brown. Dust rises, butterflies scatter, and the earth drums with their pounding hooves.

Sapphire watches, unshaken. She lowers her head to graze, tearing at the grass with measured calm. Every blade she eats feels like a decision made. Every mouthful belongs to her alone.

Most would hear only snorts and the sound of hoofbeats. But here, in the valley's breath, voices live between the sounds. Not quite speech, not quite thought. Something else. Something the wombat knows well.

Beneath the granite bank, the wombat listens and moves through earth as if it parts for him, soil closing behind his broad shoulders, roots brushing his fur like reverent fingers. In the dark, every sound carries - the thud of hooves above, the ripple of creek water against stone, and the deep hum of bees working rosemary banks. He feels them all, stitched into the soil like threads in a tapestry.

And deeper still, a shard of the crystal waits. It is not the only one - for the valley holds many pieces, scattered like seeds, each keeping part of the whole. This one lies hidden in the granite's heart, known only to the wombat.

It pulses with the rhythm of his breath, with the rhythm of the soil itself. Ochre, gold, green, silver - its colors shift like the seasons, as though the whole valley were caught in its depths.

Long ago, men searched these creeks and rivers for treasure. They bent over metal pans and cradles at Araluen Creek, chasing glimmers of gold through mud and water. They thought the riches lay in dust and nuggets, in seams that could be broken and carried away. But the wombat knew better. What shines in water is only a faint reflection of what lies deeper, older, and truer.

The shard remembers. The soil remembers. The gold was never the treasure at all.

Above the ground, the horses quarrel still - Apples. Carrots. Silence. Their voices drift down through soil and stone, and the shard holds them too, folding quarrels and whispers alike into its quiet song.

The chase ends where Moodong Creek makes a bend. From the air, the valley's secret would be clear: the creek runs like a silver ribbon until, just here, it divides. One branch carries on, steady and sure, but the other lifts away, curving upward into the next valley. Together they form two arms stretching west, two paths waiting to be chosen.

Both pintos pause at the fork, sides heaving, manes tangled with grass seeds. Louise nudges toward the narrower branch, where willows lean low across the water. Thelma nickers toward the wider stream, where reeds stand tall like watchmen.

Two paths, their voices murmur together, softer now, not quarreling but curious.

Sapphire joins them at last, stepping into the shallow water where the fork begins. Her glacier eyes fix on the narrower branch, the one locals call Appletree Creek. She lowers her head and drinks, slow and steady, as though she has chosen already.

The She Oaks whisper above, the sound falling like advice. The creek hums at their hooves, its forked waters carrying secrets upstream and down.

Beneath it all, the wombat listens, and he hears the fork as more than water. He hears it as a question, an invitation, a promise. Two paths. Two valleys. Two stories. But only one song.

Thelma flicks her ears, impatient. Apples wait there.

Louise stamps, defiant. Carrots wait here.

Sapphire only drinks, her silence stretching deeper than both choices.

The wombat shifts in his tunnel, stone and soil pressing close. He knows what lies ahead. The horses are not only quarreling. They are listening. The valley is teaching them - as it teaches all who stay long enough - that names matter, choices matter, and even quarrels carry meaning when whispered into the earth.

And still the She Oaks whisper. And still Moodong Creek hums. And still the wombat listens, holding it all in the chamber of his heart.

The Mob and the Wallaby

Dawn leans softly across the valley, the first light spilling gold over the She Oaks. Their whispers rise with the morning wind, weaving through branches, tugging at the rosemary banks that flow toward Moodong Creek. The creek hums in reply, its song steady, carrying yesterday into today.

Out in the open flats, grey kangaroos gather. A mob, quiet as cloud-shadows, grazes on the dew-heavy grass. Their heads rise and fall in unison, ears flicking, tails shifting, muscles coiled beneath fur the color of smoke. They move like a single breath, steady and unhurried, guardians of dawn and dusk.

The joeys wobble near their mothers, legs too long, tails too heavy, tumbling over roots and tussocks. Each fall is met with patience - one nudge, one steadying lick, then back on their feet. The mob holds them safe in its rhythm, as if the whole valley were teaching them how to belong.

If you stand still long enough, the valley tells you what the kangaroos are thinking. Their voices live close to the soil, half-thought, half-thunder... Steady. Wait. Watch.

The words are not loud, not spoken, but carried in the silence between ear-flicks and tail-thuds. They graze, they listen, they hold the ground as though it were their own heartbeat.

A smaller shadow keeps to the rosemary banks. There the pretty-faced wallaby lingers at the edge of light, her fur soft brown, her eyes ringed in cream. She is not bold like the kangaroos, nor loud in her silence. She belongs to the edges, to the secret places where scent and shadow meet.

She moves delicately, a whisper within whispers. Every hop is quiet, every pause precise. When she feeds, it is with care, nibbling rosemary tips as if tasting stories stored in the leaves.

Her voice, if you listen closely, is softer still... Hide. Hold. Hush.

She is the secret guardian, the one who knows how to vanish. Her presence balances the mob's strength, as silence balances thunder.

Not far from her, another figure passes - a swamp wallaby, heavier, darker, a bachelor wanderer. His movements are coarse, crashing through bracken rather than slipping between stems. His fur is shadow-black with rusty tinges, his head thick, his jaw blunt. He does not linger over rosemary; he tears at grass in mouthfuls, chewing noisily, as though daring anyone to stop him.

His voice, if the valley lets you hear it, is rough and simple... Mine. Now. Enough.

Less refined, less clever, yet still belonging. The Swamp Wallaby's voice is no whisper, no hush. He is a thud, a grunt, a half-formed thought. And even that has its place.

The pretty-faced wallaby glances once toward him, her cream-ringed eyes calm. She does not argue or flee. She simply shifts deeper into shadow, holding her silence as surely as the swamp wallaby holds his noise.

Together they paint the truth of the banks: two kinds of presence, one delicate, one blunt, each carrying a different piece of the valley's song.

Beneath them all, the wombat listens. In his burrows, the earth is cool, pressed close, breathing with him. Every shift above reaches him: the kangaroos' steady thumps, the pretty-faced wallaby's featherlight steps, the swamp wallaby's clumsy crashes through the undergrowth.

To the wombat, the differences are clear. The pretty-faced one is a ripple in the soil, a hush that barely stirs the earth. The swamp wallaby is a thud, a blunt sound that startles worms and shakes loose pebbles. One is refinement, one is roughness, but both belong. The soil makes no judgment - it carries every sound.

And deeper still, the shard listens too. Its colors turn faint silver, green, then a flash of ochre-gold, as though each note of movement has been folded inside it. The delicate hush, the coarse thud, the mob's steady thunder, even the horses' quarrels - all are held together, remembered without choosing.

The wombat knows this is how the valley keeps its song. Not one voice, not one kind of presence, but many. Rough and refined, loud and soft, fleeting and steady. All are stitched into the same remembering.

Above ground, the kangaroos lift their heads in sudden stillness. The mob holds its breath. Ears twist, noses test the air.

Thelma and Louise appear at the meadow's edge, still restless from their quarrel. Their hooves drum the ground, laughter hidden in their snorts. Apples, Thelma insists, flicking her tail. Carrots, Louise argues back.

The mob does not answer in kind. Instead, their reply is silence - long, watchful, unbroken. Steady, their voices whisper into the ground. Wait.

The wallaby shifts in the shadows, her dark eyes fixed on the pintos. Her voice is quieter still, almost lost in the creek's hum. Hush.

For a moment, the whole valley balances there - the horses quarreling, the mob holding steady, the wallaby vanishing into silence. Opposites pressed together, held by the soil, and remembered by the shard.

The wombat knows this balance. He listens as the crystal pulses with it, storing quarrel, thunder, and hush alike. The valley is never one story. It is always many. Two paths, two valleys, two stories. But one song.

And still the She Oaks whisper. And still Moodong Creek hums. And still the wombat listens, carrying it all deeper into the earth.

The Parrots and the Finches

By midday, the valley is never still. The sun hangs high, warm on stone and grass, pouring its weight down until even the shadows grow thin. The granite bank gleams with heat. The She Oaks seem to shiver though no breeze stirs them, their needles clicking faintly, like whispered complaints. Dust drifts golden above the paths where wallabies and roos had passed at dawn, holding to the air as though reluctant to fall.

The air itself shimmers with wings. First come the crimson rosellas. They burst into the branches like fireworks - streaks of crimson and cobalt flaring against the silver bark of the gums. Their calls cut the quiet with sudden sharpness, laughter and quarrel knotted together.

Their voices tumble like children tugging the same toy, stubborn and unrelenting... Mine. Mine again. Gone, gone, gone.

The branches shudder beneath them, seeds scatter, and still their clamor rises. To hear them is to listen to the valley argue with itself - loud, bright, insistent. Yet for all the noise, their feathers gleam like jewels. Chaos gilded in color.

Above the quarrel glides another presence. King parrots, regal in their deep greens and velvet-crimson chests. Their wings cut slow, deliberate strokes, rising above the mayhem with the patience of judges in a crowded court.

From their high perch in the white gum, they miss nothing: the frenzy of rosellas, the sparks of wrens, and the tides of pink finches.

Their voices are not chatter but weight, rolling low like storm clouds gathering at the edge of hearing... Too soon. Too loud.

The valley carries their meaning as a verdict, heavy as stone. Silence becomes their power, as commanding as any quarrel.

Closer to the earth, tiny flames spark. Fairy-wrens, bright as living sapphires, flit from stalk to stalk, tails cocked like banners. Their flight is a zigzag and loop, with sudden drops into the grass, then bursts skyward again - light teaching itself how to play.

Their voices scatter like quicksilver, bright fragments of thought never held for long... Here – There – Gone already.

Each note vanishes before the next is finished, a conversation made only of beginnings. Their laughter is written in motion, blue sparks stitching mischief through the meadow.

The finches gather differently still. Not in quarrels. Not in Sparks. But in tides.

At first, they are barely seen - small specks along a fence, blending into seed heads and bark. Then, without warning, the air erupts.

Sometimes it is a bronze cloud - hundreds of bronze wings rising together, their feathers flashing like coins caught in the sun. Other days it is a pink cloud - red-browed finches lifting as one, their soft blush sweeping across the sky like a petal carried on the wind. And sometimes, rarer still, it is a red cloud - crimson flashes streaking the air, a sudden storm of fire -blue.

Each flock moves as a single body, a ribbon folding and unfolding in the sky, stretching wide, then tightening, then spreading once more. The hue may change, but the shape is always the same - seamless, spellbound, unbroken.

Their voice is one voice... A single thought. A single breath. A tide of color rising and falling.

Yet not all voices rise skyward. Along the rosemary bank, the echidna shuffles slowly, nose pressed to soil, claws scratching with patient rhythm. She is spines and silence, steady as stone, unhurried by quarrel or tide. Where parrots scream and finches wheel, she simply listens to the ground and answers with her own quiet tapping. The valley translates her persistence into a voice as old as the wombat's... Slow. Steady. Keep digging.

The valley holds its breath to watch. Even the rosellas hush, the wrens pause mid-flight, the king parrots lift their solemn eyes. Kangaroos, wallabies, and even bees at the daisies seem stilled by the spectacle.

Then - as swiftly as it began - the sky is empty. The cloud has dissolved. The finches are gone.

The day wears on, the air layered with contradiction - rosella quarrels, wren sparks, finch tides, king parrot silence. It is midday music. Not harmony, not chaos. Both at once.

But as the sun tilts toward the western ridge, the music falters.

The light changes first. Shadows stretch, granite blushes pink. Bees yield to crickets. The meadow itself exhales.

The rosellas fall quiet, feathers ruffling uneasily. The wrens freeze mid-dart, their mischief swallowed whole. The finches huddle close, wings folded tight. Even the king parrots still their strokes, settling into council on the high gum branch.

And sometimes, at the edge of light, another shadow slips between stems. Its the Dingo. His paws fall silent on stone, his coat carrying dusk on its back. He does not join the quarrels or the dances; he waits. Eyes amber, fixed, unblinking, he listens with a patience sharper than hunger. The valley hears his voice differently from all others - not quarrel, not mischief, not tide... Mine... soon. A promise... A threat... Both.

Beneath the branches, deeper than quarrel and spark, louder than wings or chatter, something else hums. Not wind... Not water... Not bees.

The ground itself vibrates - a note without voice, felt in talons and tiny claws, insistent and undeniable... The rosellas shiver, and the wrens blink, hushed for once. The finches press tighter together.

And the oldest king parrot ruffles his wings. His call rolls heavy into the dusk, carried by the valley until it feels like the earth itself has spoken... The earth remembers. The dreamer stirs.

Then silence. Not peace, but waiting. The kind of pause between one heartbeat and the next.

The valley waits.

The Kookaburra and the Lyrebird

When dawn breaks, the kookaburras begin. Their laughter rolls across the valley like thunder wearing a grin - loud, sudden, impossible to ignore. Perched ragged along the gum branches, they lift their heads and cackle until the sky itself seems to split with joy.

One starts. Another answers. Then the whole chorus folds together in wild hilarity, as though time itself cannot turn a page without their command.

The kangaroos twitch their ears, muscles tightening as if ready to leap. The parrots squabble louder to compete, their bickering sharpened against the rolling mirth. Even the horses glance up from their grazing, ears flicking at the racket, eyes wide with bemused patience.

It is the kookaburras who claim the first sound of morning - always, without fail. And at dusk, they do it again. As the sun slides behind the ridge and the sky bruises purple, their chorus bursts forth, wild and unstoppable. The whole valley shakes with it, nailed into rhythm by their noise.

Their voices are blunt and unyielding... Now. Again. Begin.

They are clock-keepers. They fasten dawn and dusk with laughter that is more than laughter - a rhythm older than humor, a sound that binds the day to its edges.

When at last their throats rasp and fade, another voice rises.

From the underbrush steps the lyrebird, with feathers of muted earth browns, greys, and silver edges. Her tail unfurls like a secret. Plumes curl into filigree, crossing and bending until they form a silver fan, wide enough to catch every echo that lingers in the air.

She moves with care, each step deliberate, as though chosen long before. Her throat trembles.

The kookaburra's laughter spills out again, perfect and uncanny. The mob stiffens. Even the kookaburras falter mid-chuckle, startled by the flawless echo of themselves. But the lyrebird does not pause. She bends her song into a cockatoo's cry, then into the rush of finches, then into the hiss of grass in the wind. Every sound is hers to keep, hers to repeat. The valley is her library, and she is its archivist.

The horses snort uneasily, and the parrots mutter, affronted at being copied. The wrens dart in jittery zigzags, wondering if their chatter has already been stolen. But still the lyrebird continues her song. Her throat is a mirror polished smooth by patience. She does not invent - she gathers. She does not lead - she remembers.

Tonight, she remembers too deeply... Her tail lifts higher, plumes trembling like antennae tuned to a hidden frequency. Her song slows, deepens, drawn from another well entirely.

What rises now is not bird, not beast, not wind... It is a voice from beneath the granite bank, where roots twist like veins and the shard lies buried in its chamber of stone. A murmur not meant for daylight... Not yet. The gate breathes still.

The words fall wrong, heavy, undeniable.

The kookaburras fall silent, their dawn-and-dusk certainty splintered. The rosellas freeze. The wrens vanish into the grass without a sound. Even the creek seems to hold its tongue.

The lyrebird closes her tail with a whisper of feathers and slips back into shadow. No one speaks.

The day had begun with laughter, confident and strong, but it closed with unease. For if the kookaburras are clock-keepers, then the lyrebird is something older still.

She is not merely a mimic. She is memory itself - carrying echoes too deep for daylight. She hears the roots shifting, the stones remembering, the shard turning faint colors in its sleep. And when she chooses, she gives those sounds a voice.

The creatures of the valley sense it, though they cannot name it. The finches huddle tight on the wire. The pretty-faced wallaby edges closer to the rosemary bank, eyes fixed on the ground. Even the mob moves more heavily, tails dragging as though burdened by words.

Above them, the kookaburras stare at one another, beaks closed. Their laughter, so sure at dawn and dusk, feels brittle now - a fragile net in the face of that low murmur... The gate breathes still.

The phrase coils through branches long after the lyrebird has gone. What gate? Whose breath? No one asks aloud. The silence thickens, settling into bark, fur, and feather. It is not peace. It is waiting.

And the valley waits well... It has done so for centuries - roots steady, stones unmoving, secrets folded deep in soil.

Tonight, more keenly stirred by the mimic's warning, the lyrebird hides, with her tail tucked, and her chest still. She has given back a sound that was never hers, borrowed from the earth's hidden chamber.

And deep below, the wombat stirs in his burrow. The words brush his fur like a tremor. He does not wake. He remembers. For in the valley, nothing is ever lost.

The Lace Monitor

The valley tilts on its axis when he comes... Shadows stretch longer than they should, sliding out like indian ink poured across the flaxen grass. The air grows heavy and weighted, as though the rich red soil itself holds its breath. The meadow, bright with chatter only moments ago, folds into complete hush.

Smaller creatures vanish first. Fairy-wrens drop into stalks, their sapphire tails gone in a blink. The finches, who traced the sky in ribbons of light, dive into cover, wings pressed tight to their sides. Even the bees falter mid-flight, paths bending away, with blossoms left half-sipped.

The lace monitor enters the valley without haste. His claws strike the earth with a slow rhythm - tap, drag, tap, drag. Each step is deliberate, each pause an unspoken but real threat. His tongue flickers between movements, tasting dust and pollen, measuring the world not by sight but by scent and tremor.

His body is a scroll of old patterns - cream and black runes twisting across his back, marks that whisper of ancient fires and prey, long turned to bone. Each scale seems etched with memory, as if carved from stone.

The valley remembers him.

The rosellas then scatter into high branches, quarrels clipped short like threads cut by a sharp blade. The wrens extinguish their sparks into silence. Even the impressive king parrots circle uneasily overhead, their shadows sliding across his scales but daring no closer.

He does not chase. He does not need to. His presence alone is enough to turn noise into silence, and he knows it.

At the meadow's edge, he halts. His golden eyes, ancient and unblinking, scan the steep slope. His tongue flickers again, pulling the story of the valley into his mouth - damp earth, beetle musk, eucalyptus, the faint metallic tang of water moving under rounded stones.

He turns toward a stand of stringybark. Without pause, he begins to climb, claws carving deep grooves into the bark as if he were writing his name upon the tree. Higher he goes, body pressed close, tail dragging like a rope of muscle, anchoring, releasing, then anchoring again.

A hollow yawns above him - dark, wide enough for possums. The lace monitor's tongue flickers, sliding into shadow. The air is stale, thick with the dust of fur long vanished, and nests collapsed into silence. He leans deeper, claws hooked into the rim, then eases back. Empty.

He climbs higher still, pausing at another notch. A faint scurry stirs within - only insects. His jaw snaps once, more ritual than hunger, then he moves on, regardless, scales untroubled and unimpressed.

Below, the mob gathers uneasily in the grass... The eldest kangaroo plants its tail, muscles taut. A rumble moves through the marsupial's chest into the soil, more felt than heard. The valley translates: Stone-skin waits.

The lace monitor halts mid-climb, hearing his name, and stillness coils through his muscles. His head turns slowly, deliberately, toward the rosemary bank... There it is. The burrow.

Hidden beneath green spears and tiny blue stars, cloaked in the sharp breath of lemongrass. To most, it is herbs. To him, it is a gate. He does not see the wombat, but he knows. The dream is there. The keeper is there.

He descends, claws dragging scars down the trunk - a carving of intent. The bark remembers.

On the ground, he slides forward unhurriedly. Each step claims the soil, each flick of tongue draws the scent closer. Deep under the rosemary, beneath the lemongrass roots, something ancient hums. The shard...

He tastes it on the air - metallic, bitter-sweet, alive.

The rosemary's sharpness rises, stinging his tongue. The lemongrass bends though no breeze stirs. Bees spiral upward, their hum swelling, urgent, and protective. Shadows lean inward, pressing close, as if the valley itself braces to resist him.

The lace monitor pauses, scales rippling with breath. One claw extends and he steps onto the fringe.

The change is immediate... The hum of bees sharpens into a wall of sound. The air thickens, pressing against him. The lemongrass bends hard, as though an unseen hand pushes outward. Even the shadows crowd closer, barring his path.

The lace monitor hisses, his tongue flicking. He knows poison. He knows venom. He has swallowed rot and walked away stronger. Death has never frightened him.

But this is different... Not poison of fang or leaf. Not bitterness of carrion. This is power woven into root and stone, old as fire itself. It prickles along his scales, raising each like a blade.

He could push through. He could claw into soil, scatter rosemary, tear lemongrass, and unearth what stirs. He is built for both patience and power.

But the valley resists.

From the shadows, a voice rises... Not a bird. Not wind. Echo. The lyrebird. Unseen, yet everywhere.

Her throat shapes words not her own. Borrowed, pulled from the crystal's chamber, they roll out heavy as stone: Not for you. Not yet.

The lace monitor freezes, and his golden eyes burn. His tail flicks once, striking the earth with an intentional but dull thud.

Silence spreads. Even the bees hesitate mid-flight, caught between attack and retreat. The mob holds still, ears straining.

The lace monitor inhales, tongue tasting the boundary one last time. Then, slowly, deliberately, he turns away.

He does not flee. He does not yield. Each claw scratches defiance into the soil. His reptilian body curves, scales glinting once in fading light, before he melts away again into the shadows.

He will wait. For his waiting is as natural to him as breath.

High above, the eagles shift their wings, circling wider. Cockatoos mutter like mourners in the gums. The wrens whisper faintly in the grass but do not rise.

And the valley breathes again - thin, shallow, relieved. Yet beneath the rosemary, the soil still trembles. The dreamer still stirs.

And the lace monitor has marked the gate with his silence... Not defeated. Not gone. Only waiting.

The Red-Bellied Black Snake

She moves slowly where the grass parts, a stealthy ribbon of midnight laid upon the earth. Her body gleams black as oil, polished by sun and shadow alike, yet along her belly runs a fire-line of red - as though she carries embers hidden beneath her scales.

No hoof strikes announce her coming. No claws scratch bark. She arrives soundless, so quiet that the air itself seems to hush in deference.

The parrots do not quarrel when she slides past. Instead, their crimson feathers press close to the bark, and their heads duck nervously as though they had never argued at all. The kangaroos shift their tails, leaning well back on their haunches to give her space, muscles tense, though they dare not leap. Even the kookaburras swallow their laughter, and their grins turn brittle when the grass begins to bend in her shape.

For she is not just a snake. She is warning.

The red-bellied black knows poisons. She knows which leaf can soothe, which root can blister, which flower can heal if ground with care. She carries old knowledge, not written in words but kept in fangs and silence. She knows death, and she knows how silence cuts sharper than fangs.

Her tongue flickers endlessly as she glides forward, tasting the threads of scent braided through the meadow. Kangaroo sweat... Cockatoo feathers... Dust... Sun-warmed granite... But above all, she notes a sharp spike of rosemary and the citrus tang of lemongrass.

She approaches the burrow's gate, that hidden mouth beneath the curtain of herbs, but she does not enter. No serpent ever has. The herbs bristle deliberately against her presence, their oils sharp in the air, a burning perfume wall, its invisible yet certain presence.

Still, she lingers.

The bees rise in uneasy circles, their hum thickening into a spell that vibrates against her scales. The lemongrass sways, though no wind stirs. The rosemary's blue stars seem to tremble, pulsing with the wombat's dreaming breath.

The snake coils back, her body folding upon itself, black loops layered like shadows stacked. Her head lifts, her eyes black as polished obsidian, unblinking, holding the horizon in their glassy depths. She hisses once, low and drawn, and the sound creeps into roots, into hollows, into every waiting ear.

A spider crosses her path - small, spindly, carrying its own quiet poison in its fragile body. She lowers her head until her tongue brushes the web it trails behind, tasting the silk.

When the gate fails, she whispers to the spider, call me.

The spider stills, as though hearing a command older than silk itself. It vanishes into the bark, unseen but not forgotten.

Nearby, the wallaby twitches at the edge of the meadow, fur bristling, ears sharp. The mob shifts uneasily, tails thudding the earth. Above, a black cockatoo shrieks, the sound splitting the air like torn cloth, its cry falling heavy across the valley.

The snake does not strike, and does not need to, as her promise is enough.

She slides onward, her scales parting grass with the faint hiss of dry leaves rubbed together. Behind her, the meadow remembers her passing. The stalks are pressed flat, a secret road burned into green.

Yet even in her absence, her presence lingers.

The herbs whisper louder, their scent biting. The bees patrol tighter, their circles sharp, their hum rising toward frenzy. The lemongrass leans inward, blades like spears bent in a single direction - toward the burrow.

All this aside, the wombat sleeps on beneath the soil - his dreams move slow, thick as mud.

Safe, bound, breathing still. But danger has marked his gate.

And danger waits.

Night thickens, and with it the power of her silence. Owls stir in the gums, their golden eyes tracking, but they make no call. Moths flicker in the dark, drawn to flowers, only to veer sharply away from the path she has left. Even the frogs at the creek grow still when her shadow nears the water's edge.

She is silence given form, and silence has weight.

The local mob of kangaroos resumes grazing only when she has gone, and even then, their ears tilt constantly, listening, expecting her return. The wallaby will not come near the rosemary bank tonight; she crouches in the shadow of a large boulder, eyes wide, tail coiled beneath her, trembling at sounds only she hears.

The cockatoos, restless, take wing as a flock, their white forms blotting the dusk sky, their voices harsh. But they do not settle near the lemongrass. They choose a further tree, as if distance were safety.

The lyrebird does not sing... not tonight, but she hides her tail and waits in silence, for she knows the snake's hiss is a sound not meant to be imitated.

Now, the valley itself seems stretched thin - each breath shallow, each sound restrained.

The snake glides on, unhurried, with her belly pressed against the earth, reading the land the way others read stars or leaves. She knows where roots twist, where burrows lie, where stones warm in sunlight. Each flick of her tongue writes the valley's story onto her body.

She knows poisons.

The bitter stem of the nightshade curls low near the fence line. The milk of the spurge is sharp enough to blind. The honey-sweet nectar of the grevillea is harmless until fermented in still water.

She knows healing.

The bark of the tea-tree, where sap dries into medicine. The juice of the aloe, seeping cool against burns. The leaf of the plantain is ground beneath the fang and spit to draw out the sting.

In her scales lies an old catalogue - not of letters or ink, but of memory and taste, of venom and cure. She has carried this knowledge longer than the eagles have circled, longer than the rosellas have quarreled. It is hers by inheritance, hers by survival.

And so she waits.

Not with hunger, but with certainty.

Back at the rosemary bank, the herbs bristle even after her leaving. Their scent thickens in the night, resinous, bitter, almost painful in the nostrils. Bees cluster closer to the blossoms, wings a constant hum. The lemongrass bends so far it seems nearly broken, its blades trembling though the night air lies still.

And the wombat dreams on. For now, his sleep is unbroken; his breath is a slow, steady drumbeat. Yet in his dream, perhaps he hears the hiss that crept through the soil. Perhaps he stirs once, curling deeper.

The valley listens with him.

Every branch, every blade of grass, every hollow root holds the echo of her passing... Not for now. Not yet. But danger waits.

And the red-bellied black remembers.

The Eagles and the Black Cockatoos

The valley belongs to the sky as much as to the soil.

High above the ridges, the wedge-tailed eagles circle. Their wings carve shadows vast enough to swallow a mob of kangaroos whole. They do not flap so much as glide, riding invisible rivers of wind, silent and unhurried. Their feathers catch the sunlight, gold on the edges, bronze where the air thickens, so they seem crowned by fire.

When they pass, every creature below takes notice.

The horses lift their heads, ears twitching, eyes bright and wary. The wallaby freezes mid-chew, grass still clamped between her teeth. The rosellas, quarrelsome at any other hour, still their chatter, feathers pressed close, waiting to see whether the eagles descend.

They rarely do.

The eagles are not hunters here. They are sentinels, and look not for prey but for change, reading the valley as though it were a map only their eyes can see. They know the slip of heat rising from stone, the curve of currents where air bends, and the faint disruptions that ripple upward from soil that has been disturbed.

From his highest circle, the eldest eagle speaks - not with sound, but with the low pulse of presence that only the sky can carry... The rhythm falters.

His shadow sweeps across the meadow. Below, Thelma and Louise stamp nervously, their quarrels forgotten, their tails flicking.

Even Sapphire, steady and slow, raises her head to watch, with her icy blue eyes narrowed against the light.

Another eagle tilts her wings and answers, voice deep as thunder rolling behind mountains...He stirs again.

Her interpreted words ripple downward with the sweep of her shadow.

Far below, in the She Oaks, the black cockatoos stir.

They rise in a burst of dark wings, their cries raw and piercing. Where the rosellas chatter like quarrelsome children, the black cockatoos wail like mourners at a grave. Their voices are long, drawn-out laments, carrying grief across ridges, through branches, and then onward down the creek. Each cry is a tear in the air, ragged and sharp.

Their calls echo, rattling along the creek through stone and hollow, until even the water seems to shiver. The dragonflies scatter, and the bees falter mid-flight. The magpies fall silent, their flutes broken in their throats.

At the rosemary's edge, the wallaby presses close. Her whiskers tremble, her paws twitch against the soil. The question rises in her chest, not spoken aloud but carried like scent through the grass: Why do they cry so?

The eldest kangaroo flicks his tail, eyes fixed on the sky. A low rumble stirs in his chest, rolling through the earth beneath them. The valley hears his answer: Not for what is, but for what will be.

The wallaby shivers, her tail thumping softly against the ground, as though the words had settled into her bones.

Above them, the cockatoos wheel. Their wings cut through sunlight, scattering black feathers that drift downward like ash across the blue. Their cries overlap, one upon another, until grief becomes a storm. It is not a song. It is a dirge.

The rosellas mutter nervously, unable to understand but unwilling to mock. Even the kookaburras, boldest of all, hold their laughter in their throats, their eyes following the black wings.

The eagles keep circling, silent again now, but their silence is not emptiness. It is weight. Their shadows tell the truth. Their eyes, sharper than any stone blade, pierce through the valley's quiet and find the tremor below.

Something shifts in the valley's breath.

The laughter of the kookaburras is late that night. The lyrebird does not sing. Even the bees patrol with sharper urgency, darting faster between the rosemary stars, their hum clipped and hurried.

The wombat dreams on, but his dream is lighter now, closer to waking. The earth above him seems thinner, fragile, as though the barrier between dream and day is wearing through. The soil that once held him firm now pulses faintly, like skin stretched too far.

The cockatoos cry until their voices rasp. Their wings tire, their flight slows, yet still they call, their grief pouring into branches and stones, a lament no creature can ignore.

The eagles hold their silence. They do not comfort. They do not mourn. They only watch, their circles steady, their wings unbroken.

And all who live in the valley know: the sky itself has spoken.

The message is now clear, though no words are given.

Dawn and dusk no longer pass unbroken. The rhythm falters and the dreamer stirs.

The cockatoos cry for tomorrow... The eagles wait for it... And the valley listens.

The Rosemary Cloak

At the valley's heart, where soil meets stone and the air tastes sharp with green, the burrow lies hidden. Few know the way. None will enter uninvited.

It is cloaked in prostrate rosemary - bushes low and tangled, their flowing branches crowned with blue blossoms like tiny stars. The scent rises strong, piercing, a perfume of memory and defense. To brush against it is to wake every nerve, as though the plant itself commands:... Stay aware. Stay back.

Either side of it grows lemongrass sentinels, blades long and bright, spears thrust upward, glinting silver when the moon touches them. Their scent is sharp as cut air, cleansing and biting all at once - a breath that scours the lungs clean. Together, rosemary and lemongrass weave a living gate - a wall both fragrant and fierce.

The bees know this gate best.

They drift from blossom to blossom, golden bodies dusted in pollen, wings glinting in the sun. To the careless eye, they are only busy with their work, but the valley knows better. They are listeners, messengers, and carriers of whispers.

Each bee pauses longer on the blossoms that touch the burrow's edge. They press their legs into petals, as though collecting not just pollen but words. They move from rosemary star to lemongrass spear, weaving an invisible thread of sound that hums in harmony with the wombat's dream.

Still dreaming, one bee murmurs through its wings, in the deep tone only bees know. Still breathing, hums another, wings thrumming.

But not for long, answers a third, in tonal unison, lifting into the sunlight.

The kangaroos pause at the meadow's edge to watch. Their ears tilt forward, their tails thump once against the ground. The wallaby lingers too, nose twitching, caught between curiosity and fear. Even Sapphire, the aloof horse, stops grazing when the bees circle lower, their hum sharpened like a warning bell.

The lace monitor has felt this wall and turned aside... The snake has lingered and slid away... But the bees never leave... They are constant.

At dawn, when kookaburras shatter the silence with laughter, the bees are already on their guard. At midday, when the sun pounds heat into granite and the parrots quarrel in fevered bursts, the bees hum steadily, their rhythm never broken. At dusk, when cockatoos wail and shadows stretch purple across the meadow, the bees remain.

They crawl deeper into the blossoms, vanishing into the rosemary's shadow, as though guarding the wombat's breath itself. Some carry messages back to the hive tucked beneath a fallen log - reports of tremors in the soil, shifts in the herbs' scent, or the faint pulse of air that seems to breathe upward from beneath the ground. Their dances are not only for nectar; they map the heartbeat of the valley itself.

Other creatures take note.

The rosellas, noisy at any other hour, grow strangely subdued near the rosemary. They tilt their heads, uncertain, unwilling to quarrel within earshot of the bees' hum. The fairy-wrens dare not flit through the blossoms, though they dance in every other thicket. Even the cockatoos, bold and brash, do not land within the lemongrass. They circle once overhead and choose another tree.

The herbs stand tall, woven thick, but it is the bees that turn the cloak into a living shield. Their hum threads into the soil, binding the roots together, weaving scent into sound, defense into dream.

And beneath them, in soil knotted with roots and memory, the wombat dreams on, his breath moves the earth like a tide, and his heart keeps time with bees' wings.

Sometimes the soil shifts faintly, a tremor that presses upward. The herbs respond at once - rosemary bristling, lemongrass bending as though struck by sudden wind. The bees surge into the air, spiraling, their hum loud and fierce, until the tremor settles again. Then they return to their blossoms, patient, resolute, as if nothing had disturbed them.

The mob of kangaroos watches these moments with solemn eyes, and outward thoughts... The gate breathes, drifts upward from the eldest roo, though softly, as if reluctant to think it too near. The wallaby shuffles back, fur raised, and dares not come closer.

The horses keep their distance. Thelma and Louise argue loudly in other corners of the meadow, but neither steps near the rosemary bank. Only Sapphire turns her gaze upon it now and then, her blue eyes steady, unreadable.

The eagles circle high above, their shadows sweeping the herbs, but they never dive. The cockatoos cry at dusk, but their voices fall short of the cloak. Even the lace monitor, who once pressed his claw against the boundary, lingers far away now.

For all the valley senses what the bees know: the burrow is not asleep, not entirely... The wombat's dream is changing.

The earth seems thinner above him, stretched tight like skin over water. The herbs stand firm, yet their scent grows stronger each day, as though forced to work harder to contain what stirs beneath. The bees hum louder, circling deeper into the blossoms, wings flashing silver at twilight.

The valley does not yet know whether his waking will bring ruin or renewal. Some fear the soil will crack open, roots torn apart. Others whisper that his rising may bring balance, strength, the return of something long withheld... But for now, the herbs hold fast. And the bees remain.

Their song is constant, a low vibration threaded through air and root, carrying the promise of order... Safe. Bound. Dreaming still.

The Singing Spring and Appletree Creek

T ucked beside the rosemary's trailing veil, where stone and shadow keep their quiet counsel, the valley's creatures pause to drink from the spring that slips downhill - a hidden ribbon of water winding its way toward the wandering Moodong Creek.

It begins high in the valley as a silver thread, no wider than a hand, trickling over red granite and pale roots. Yet the sound it makes is more than water... It is music... The spring sings.

Its voice is soft, like glass struck gently, or breath moving through a reed flute. Notes tumble over stone, weaving melodies too ancient for words. At first, it is only background - the kind of sound one grows used to without noticing. But if you linger, if you give it more than passing attention, the song reveals itself. There are patterns, recurring like a chorus. There are pauses, like breaths. And there are phrases - songs stitched from the earth's memory.

At dawn, the melody is light, trilling like the wings of many wrens. By noon, when the sun weighs heavily on granite, its voice deepens to a hollow flute echo. And at dusk, when the shadows stretch long and the cockatoos cry, the spring lowers into a soft hum, steady as a drum hidden under the soil.

Birdsong falters when the spring lifts its voice. Wrens tilt their heads, tails flicking time to a melody only they can almost hear. A wallaby leans closer, whiskers trembling, ears quivering to catch the thread. Even the bees lower their flight, their hum folding into the tune until it becomes one choir.

From near the burrow's mouth, the water seeps, gathers, and slips downhill - a narrow runlet stitching its way toward Moodong Creek. The creek meanders through meadow and shade, sliding past boulders furred with moss. At the valley's end, it braids itself with Appletree Creek, that silver cousin from the next valley, carrying whispers no boundary can hold.

The horses drink warily. Thelma gulps first - greedy, loud - then jerks back when a note rises beneath her muzzle. Louise follows, slow but sure, stamping once as if the water had laughed at her reflection. Sapphire comes last. Her glacier eyes look not at the surface but into it, as though she might read the song itself. She snorts, shakes her mane, steps back, solemn.

Night lays moonlight across the spring, and it glows - names flicker like fireflies: some of creatures long gone, some not yet born. Time means nothing here; the water carries every whisper equally.

Above, the She Oaks murmur, their needled branches rustling counsel. Water carries whispers. Names grow where the apples fall.

By the creek's curve, an apple tree leans low, roots knotted in the bank, gripping soil and stone. Its branches sag with fruit. Many apples fall, rolling into the shallows to drift away, bobbing and spinning until the current hides them downstream.

One apple lies differently. Caught in the reeds, it glows as though lit from within, skin red-gold, brighter than moonlight allows. The horses sniff and recoil, nostrils flaring. The wallaby twitches her nose but does not touch. Even the cockatoos, greedy for fruit, circle once and veer away.

The apple bobs, its light pulsing with the wombat's sleeping breath. Sapphire watches last longest. She lowers her head, breath steaming in the cool air, then snorts, turns sharply, and will not look again.

The mob gathers, uneasy. A joey presses his nose to his mother's pouch and thinks, Why does it shine so?

From the eldest kangaroo, a thought moves like buried thunder: It beats with the dreamer's breath. That is reason enough.

Cockatoos shriek, scattering black feathers across the water. Rosellas mutter, quarrels muted. Kookaburras laugh, but their sound is clipped and uneasy. Even the bees thicken their circle above the rosemary veil, wings trembling as though bracing for a storm.

The spring sings louder, its tune running along roots, seeping into hollows, riding the creek like a message. Moodong Creek carries it down-valley to where Appletree Creek joins the song.

No creature downstream knows the source, yet all who drink feel a shiver in their bones - a memory not their own.

Still, the apple glows, its light deepening as each note of the spring feeds it.

The wallaby flicks her tail. What does it mean? No one answers.

The She Oaks sigh once more: Names grow where the apples fall. When the gate opens, the water will choose. Their voices drift on, carried by the creek, seeking ears beyond the valley.

Eagles wheel high and silent, shadows brushing the surface. The lace monitor watches, golden eyes unblinking. The red-bellied black coils near the bank, tongue tasting the apple's distant glow. None come closer.

Beneath it all, the wombat dreams on, his breath stirring soil and herb, shaking tiny blossoms. Each pulse matches the apple's glow - a slow, relentless drumbeat the valley cannot ignore.

Cockatoos cry again, their mourning calls scraping the night. Wrens fall silent.

All listen to the water, the apple, the dream...

The spring sings. It sings of memory. It sings of names. It sings of what will come.

And the valley listens - knowing the song is both lullaby and summons.

The Keeper's Silence

Dusk presses down, soft at first, then heavy. The valley slows. The light folds itself across the meadow like a blanket of smoke and honey. Shadows spill long and purple from the granite outcrops, draping the rosemary veil in twilight. The scent of the herbs grows sharper as the air cools, their oils rising strong and pungent, wrapping the burrow in a cloak that even darkness cannot pierce.

The horses, usually restless for carrots, stand still at the meadow's edge. Their ears flatten, their eyes gleam wide, and their tails hang motionless. Thelma and Louise, who quarrel with every breath, do not bicker now. Even Sapphire, who seems to know silence better than most, lowers her head and holds her breath as though she is listening for something only she can hear.

The kangaroos halt mid-graze, their tails anchored like spears, their muzzles lifted to catch the scent of the evening air. Their chests rise and fall in unison, breaths measured, eyes trained on the rosemary bank.

The parrots and wrens, who can never keep silent long, tuck their heads beneath their wings. The cockatoos perch like pale ghosts in the She Oaks, their crests flat, their cries swallowed whole. Even the insects slow, their droning thinned to near silence.

All sound falters except for the spring's quiet song... The burrow breathes.

So faint at first it could be mistaken for wind, the earth rises and falls with a rhythm older than stone. Rosemary shivers. Lemongrass bends. Bees spiral lower, forming a circle above the gate, their wings shimmering with the last scraps of daylight. The hum they weave is low, steady, a mantra older than words.

The stillness deepens. It is not fear that holds them silent, but reverence.

Then - a shift. From the Rosemary's shadow, a shape stirs.

First, only the gleam of his eyes: small, starlit, and unblinking. Then the curve of his fur, red-ochre, and thick, bristling against the evening light. His shape is broad, low, and powerful. Soil clings to his flanks, crumbling in slow cascades as he pushes forward.
The wombat steps halfway into view, paws pressing earth that remembers his weight.

The wallaby gasps, breath sharp in her chest. A whisper leaks from her as if against her will:

he remembers the first fire, and he hides its name.

No one answers her.

The wombat does not speak. His silence carries more weight than any call. He blinks once, deliberate, and slow as stone. His nose twitches, drawing in the air heavy with Rosemary, lemongrass, bees, and the singing spring. He sniffs again, tasting the layers of scent as though testing their truth.

His gaze lingers on the glowing apple caught in the reeds, its light pulsing in time with his breath. The apple flickers brighter as he stares, the water rippling faintly around it, as if bowing beneath his attention. The wombat does not move closer, but his presence alone is enough to charge the fruit with fire.

The valley leans toward him. Every root, every wing, every hoof seems tethered to his heartbeat. Even the She Oaks sigh more slowly, their whispers stretching long through the valley like prayers. The eagles wheel high, wings locked, moonlight shadows sliding across the meadow in steady circles.

The mob shuffles back a pace, not from fear but from awe. The eldest kangaroo bows his head, and the thought rumbles through him like stone: the keeper wakes. Yet none dare echo him aloud.

For a moment, the valley feels smaller, pulled inward, as though all its edges have bent toward this one place.

Then, just as slowly, the wombat retreats.

He does not rush. He does not falter. He simply turns, shoulders shifting like boulders sliding back into place, and steps into the Rosemary's arms. The herbs sway shut behind him, their scent rising thick, sealing the air. The bees tighten their circle once more, humming as though stitching the cloak closed. The soil exhales, settling into its long, slow breath again.

The glowing apple dims, its pulse fading to a soft ember. Yet its glow remains - not gone, only patient.

No one moves until night has fully fallen.

The kookaburras, usually quick to cackle at twilight, laugh late - their voices cracking, uncertain, too loud, as if to banish the sacred weight that still clings to the air. Their chorus stumbles, laughter breaking into jagged fragments that echo strangely in the hollows. The lyrebird does not sing at all. She folds her tail tight, eyes glinting in shadow, and keeps her silence as though guarding it.

The wombat's silence lingers, heavier than sound. It drapes over fur, feather, scale, and stone alike, pressing every creature into reflection. None can shake it. Even those who turn away find the hush clinging to their steps, following them into the night.

The She Oaks murmur once more, their voices low, branches bowing: the keeper has shown his weight. The gate shall not hold forever.

The spring softens its song, the melody dimming into a lullaby too fragile to last. The creek carries its whisper away, into Appletree Creek, into lands unseen. But here, at the heart of the valley, silence reigns.

The valley knows what it means: the keeper has revealed himself. The dream is closer to ending. The crystal waits beneath, buried and patient, but its call grows louder. And the choice it demands will not sleep forever.

The Midnight Wombat

Midnight comes like a held breath. The moon balances on the ridge, white and full, its light spilling across Eucalypt trunks and granite bank alike. The creek lies still, silver as a blade. Even the spring lowers its song, as though every note must bow to silence.

The valley inhales - and time stops.

From the rosemary veil, the wombat emerges. Not halfway. Not hidden. Entirely.

He steps into the moonlight, fur bristling with red ochre, back broad as stone. His eyes catch the white gum's glow, reflecting it back like twin stars. Around him, lemongrass spears bend low, rosemary blossoms open wide, and the bees hover in a trembling halo.

Every creature halts. The horses stand shoulder to shoulder, no quarrel between them. The pintos, so often squabbling, now stand like carved figures, ears flat, tails still. Sapphire lowers her head in a rare bow, her glacier-blue eyes unblinking.

The kangaroos bow too. The eldest roo lifts his muzzle just enough to rumble once, low, chest-deep, like thunder waiting inside stone. The mob answers in silence.

The wallaby kneels without knowing why, its small paws pressed into the earth, its whiskers trembling with awe.

Birds fold into stillness. Rosellas, who would usually quarrel over a single seed, make no sound. Fairy-wrens freeze like sparks in midair. Even the king parrots, regal watchers of the valley, remain unmoving, eyes glinting but voices sealed.

The lace monitor does not even flick his tongue, and the red-bellied black, hidden in reeds, coils tighter, her body rigid as iron. Neither predator nor prey dares stir.

The wombat walks slowly and deliberately, its path a circuit around the burrow. Each pawstep thuds with the weight of centuries. The ground beneath him seems to pulse in time with his stride - the very heartbeat of the valley.

The She Oaks cannot keep silent. Their branches creak, voices threading through the night air: One more breath. Then comes the choice.

The wombat does not answer.

He moves to the spring, dipping his muzzle close to the glowing water. Names shimmer across its surface, bright as sparks, fading at his touch. The music shifts, bending around him, folding into chords too low for birds or beasts to hear.

He turns toward the apple caught in the reeds. Its glow pulses faster now, urgent, eager to be claimed. It trembles against the current as though longing for his grasp. But he does not claim it.

Instead, he looks skyward... The eagles wheel in slow arcs above, wings vast as the night. Their silence is sharper than any cry, an eerie omen carved in shadow.

The cockatoos cry once - a single note, mournful and low, torn from their throats like cloth ripped down the seam.

The wombat blinks, unshaken. His gaze is not for the sky, not for the water, not for the apple. It is for something deeper, below all things, where roots entwine with memory.

He completes his circuit, returning to the rosemary veil. He pauses, body half in shadow, half in moonlight. The valley leans forward, waiting for sound, for decree, for anything.

But the wombat speaks only in silence, and his eyes, gleaming with moonfire, are enough. In his eyes lies the memory and the promise of choice, of the first fire, the echo of floods, and the scars of stone splitting open. Choice - not yet spoken, but already alive.

When he steps back into the burrow, the earth exhales. Time moves again.

The spring resumes its song, tentative at first, then swelling with renewed voice. The kookaburras laugh too late, their chorus jagged, uneasy, like actors missing their cue. Rosellas quarrel nervously, their bickering hollow. Kangaroos graze as though nothing had happened, though their ears flick toward the veil.

The wallaby remains kneeling long after the others rise, her body shaking as though she has touched something too large to understand. The bees then spiral lower, clinging to blossoms as if anchoring themselves against a storm not yet broken.

The apple glows on in the reeds, brighter now, its rhythm stronger, tethered to the wombat's retreat. Each pulse feels closer, faster, as though the dreamer's silence has only tightened the drumbeat.

The She Oaks whisper once more, softer, almost tender: The keeper has walked. The gate will open. What waits will bind itself to breath and bone.

The wombat does not emerge again. But his silence lingers, heavier than sound, and draped across the valley like a second nightfall.

Every heart in the valley knows: something has shifted. The Midnight Wombat has walked. The valley has felt his pulse, and the choice waits beneath the soil, glowing like a secret flame.

No one knows what will wake with him next.

The Hidden Crystal

Deep beneath the red granite bank, past roots twisted like veins, lies the chamber no paw or claw has entered in living memory. The wombat alone knows the way.

He moves through the earth as if it parts willingly for him, soil closing behind his broad shoulders, roots brushing his fur like reverent fingers. His claws scrape softly, not tearing but shaping, carving a tunnel smooth as river stone. Pebbles tumble and settle, dust drifts and resettles, but the wombat's stride is sure, steady, practiced.

The air grows cooler the deeper he goes, damp with the memory of rain long past. The scent is thick - clay, iron, sap bleeding faintly from the roots - and woven into it all is a pulse, faint at first but growing stronger. A heartbeat, not his own.

His breath keeps time with the valley above - every inhale drawing in the hum of bees, every exhale sending it back as pulse. With each breath, the earth seems to shift closer around him, as though urging him forward.

He descends into the dark until the air itself begins to glow.

At the chamber's heart rests a piece of the daffodil crystal.

It does not sit like treasure in a king's chest. It does not jut out like a weapon from the soil. It rests as though it has always belonged - a stone that dreamed itself into light.

The crystal's surface is not sharp but smooth, shaped by time and the ebb and flow of pressure. Its glow is not blinding but steady, pulsing with the rhythm of the wombat's breath, and the rhythm of the soil itself.

Within it, colors shift: ochre, gold, deep green, faint silver - as though the whole valley, every leaf and wing and hoofbeat, were caught in its heart.

The wombat settles before it, his massive body blocking the narrow passage. His fur flickers with the crystal's light, casting shadows like ancient glyphs across the stone. For a moment, it seems the walls themselves are inscribed, each mark alive, each groove remembering.

He does not touch it. He does not need to. The crystal knows him well, and he knows it. Guardian and guarded, each bound to the other by breath.

Aboveground, the She Oaks whisper, their voices slipping down through roots and soil like a chorus descending into the chamber:

Another will come. Not keeper, but seeker. Her paws are not yet here, yet her breath already stirs the dust of other paths.

The wombat lowers his head and closes his eyes. For the briefest moment, the chamber widens beyond stone, and he glimpses a valley where the She Oaks bend to whisper names, where children press their ears to the bark and hear what the earth remembers. He sees paws - small, steadfast - carrying light forward through shadow.

In the crystal's glow, other shapes shimmer - kings and queens, fair folk and hidden wonders - flickering like stories half-remembered, but not yet told. Past and future fold together like leaves drifting on the same current. And deeper still within the crystal's glow, another image flickers – a crooked staff etched with golden runes, held aloft in a cave where the walls themselves glimmer with shards of light.

The crystal answers with silence - but silence here is not empty. It is full, layered with echoes of floods and fires, seeds breaking open, wings lifting, names spoken in reverence and names forgotten - and names not yet born upon the air.

Every root above trembles with the weight of it. The kangaroos lift their heads from grazing, tails tightening. The wallaby flinches as though struck, her nose quivering, paws pressed to the earth. The horses stamp nervously, nostrils wide. The parrots hush, their chatter bitten off mid-quarrel. Even the wrens, never still, freeze in the grass, tiny blue sparks gone dull.

From the shadows, the lace monitor stirs, tail dragging against bark, eyes glowing with hunger he cannot name. The red-bellied snake slides silently over fallen leaves, her body moving in time with the pulse she feels in her bones.

Above the ridges, the eagles wheel lower, their silence sharpened. The cockatoos cry their dirge, one long rising wail that echoes down the valley until the stone itself seems to answer.

The bees hum louder, weaving furious spirals around the rosemary veil. The spring sings higher, its notes tumbling into urgency, into warning.

All know something waits beneath, locked in silence and light...

The wombat opens his eyes again, and for the briefest moment, they burn with the crystal's glow. His gaze seems not his own but borrowed - an ancient fire looking outward through a mortal body. The chamber shivers with the sight.

The She Oaks murmur again: The keeper watches. The seeker comes. The gate will not hold forever. What whispers in one valley will be spoken in another.

The wombat does not argue. He does not agree. He simply breathes, and the crystal breathes with him.

The crystal dims, not extinguished but veiled, its light seeping faintly into the roots, enough to remind the valley it is still there. Sufficient to unsettle sleep.

At length, he turns. His bulk shifts through the narrow passage, each step deliberate, claws finding the path by memory alone. Behind him, the chamber folds again into quiet, completely sealed, but the roots remember.

The crystal hums still, joined to others scattered in caverns across this valley and in other forgotten lands. And in one such distant cave, a wizard named Fozzel waits, listening for the footsteps of the seeker – a girl whose story begins where this one ends. The wombat continues his slow exit, sealing the way as he goes. Soil collapses in gentle waves, roots knitting back into place. Soon, there is no sign of a passage, no sign of a chamber - only earth, whole again.

Yet silence lingers.

Aboveground, the kangaroos shift uneasily. The wallaby presses close to the mob. The horses stand flank to flank. Birds refuse to quarrel. The bees cling tighter to blossoms. Even the kookaburras delay their dawn laugh, as though unwilling to shatter the stillness too soon.

The wombat emerges at last beneath the rosemary veil, its back dusted with soil, its breath deep and measured. He does not look back. He does not need to. The valley itself carries the memory of where he has been... For now:

The crystal sleeps. The wombat keeps. And the valley waits.

But the roots remember, and the seeker is already on her way.

Author's Note

This story began, quite quietly, with a pause. A pause by Moodong Creek, where granite glows red at dusk, where roots twist like veins into the soil, and where silence hums with more than emptiness. A place where the earth itself remembers - holding fires, floods, and footsteps deep beneath its skin.

The Midnight Wombat of Moodong Creek is part history, part dream, and entirely grounded in reverence - for the animals that move unseen, for the land that holds them, and for the mysteries that run deeper than maps. The wombat, patient and steadfast, is not imagined. He is real. His burrows shape the valley as surely as rivers and rain.

The creatures you'll meet may belong to story, but the pulse beneath the earth is true. The creek is true. And the silence - if you listen long enough - speaks.

Some truths rise easily, like stones warmed in the sun. Others must be dug for, carried carefully to the surface. This book is a remembering of both.

Thank you for listening to the earth within me.

Kerry Anne Boer

Author & Keeper of the Burrows

A Warm Invitation

Dear Wonderful Reader,

Thank you deeply for journeying with me through the pages of this book. Every word was written with you in mind - crafted to inspire, comfort, or simply bring joy into your day.

If this book has touched your heart, made you smile, or gently enriched your life, would you consider sharing your thoughts in a brief review?

Your words hold extraordinary power - not only do they help others find the book, but they also inspire me profoundly as an author, guiding and nurturing my creative path forward.

It would mean the world to me if you took just a moment to leave your honest reflections. Whether a few words or several lines, every review makes an enormous difference.

To leave your review, please visit the book's page on Amazon. https://www.amazon.com/review/review -your-purchases/?asin=BOOKASIN

Thank you, from the bottom of my heart, for your time, kindness, and support.

With warmth and wonder,

Kerry Anne Boer

www.ingramcontent.com/pod-product-compliance
Lightning Source LLC
Chambersburg PA
CBHW060353180626
46817CB00008B/2997